Watch Out
for the
Crocodile

Lisa Moroni & Eva Eriksson

Watch Out
for the
Crocodile

GECKO PRESS

"We're going! We're going!" Tora shouts, running round the house like a wild thing.

It's the first day of Dad's vacation and they're going camping.

It's about time they did something fun, Tora thinks. All Dad does is work, drink coffee, sit at the computer, and talk on his cell phone. He is a very boring father.

But now at last they're off to the forest to see some wild animals!

"First we need to buy groceries," Dad says. "There are no shops in the forest."

Tora groans. In the forest they should be cavemen, living on berries and mushrooms. But her father goes shopping anyway.

Boring Dad!

Shopping takes up half the day. Then they have to get in the car and drive. Forever!

Why is the forest so far away? When Tora grows up she's going to live there.

At last they're in the forest.
But where are all the wild animals?
"You have to look very carefully," Dad says.
"They're not always easy to find."

Tora looks everywhere, but
she doesn't see a single animal.
Dad's looking at his GPS,
so he doesn't either.

Then, right when Tora spies a tiny baby
ant, Dad calls out:
   "Look up there—see that woodpecker?"
   "Where, where?" says Tora.
   "There, there!" Dad points it out.

But Tora can't see it.
"It flew away," says Dad.
Stupid bird, thinks Tora.
And now the ant's gone, too.

But then Tora sees a snake!
It must be a boa constrictor, or
maybe an anaconda. Anyway, it's huge
and winding right across the path.
How will they get past?

"It's just a root," laughs Dad. He steps over the snake and he's not even scared.
Silly Dad!

Then he sees something else. A squirrel!
"Where, where, where?" asks Tora.
"There! Over in the birch tree.
Don't you see it?"
No, Tora doesn't see the squirrel, not
even through the binoculars. Because she's
seen something completely different…

...a flock of giraffes, stretching their necks to eat leaves.

Dad misses them because he's
talking on his cell phone.
And then he misses the…

...lion lying in wait on the plains.

Then silly old Dad is right there, saying there might be thistles and spiders. He frightens the lion away.

"Come and have a look at these stones," he says.

"What stones?" Tora mutters. "They're not stones, they're…"

"…sunbathing hippopotamuses."
They'd be really cross if she climbed up on them.
Tora thinks probably they should keep going and leave the hippos in peace.

Suddenly Dad stops and sighs. He says that
when he was little there was a troll forest here.
But now there are only tree stumps.

Tora looks around.

"Are you sure they're stumps, Dad? Can't you
see that they're actually…

…trolls?"

Dad shakes his head. He can't see any trolls.

Tora plays with the troll children and throws sticks for their wild dog. But she can't play for long because Dad wants to keep going.

"We'll set up our camp once we're through this fog," he says.

Tora rushes ahead, because she knows who likes fog…

Fairies, of course! The fog makes them dance.
"Tora, wait! Don't go too far!"
Dad sounds a little scared. Then his voice disappears
in the fog. Tora does, too. Everything disappears.
Tora can't see the fairies or Dad any more—only fog!
Now she is a bit scared.

Luckily, right then, Tora finds her father again.
Now they just need to cross a river, which Dad
calls a stream.

"We'll walk across that log," he says. "Easy as pie."

Tora stares at the brown water. Has Dad gone crazy?
That's not a log, that's…

…a crocodile! A river crocodile with a craving
for crunchy child-legs!

"You can do it," says Dad. "You're very good at jumping."

Tora hesitates…but luckily she's a good jumper, and fast as well.

She jumps.
And—yes! She's made it!
But oh, no! The crocodile wants tough old Dad-legs today!
"Help!" yells poor Dad.

Tora has to save him. She fights off the crocodile while Dad makes it to shore.

Then the crocodile gets furious! It lunges at Tora. But just as she's about to be eaten alive, her father pulls her to safety.

That was close!

At last, they arrive. Lucky they bought those groceries! When you've been fighting hungry crocodiles, a hot dog is exactly what you need.

Out on the lake the water glistens, mysterious and beautiful. Tora wonders if anyone lives on the island in the middle of the lake.

"But Tora, that's not an island," says Dad. "Can't you see what it is?"

Tora looks again and sees that it's not an island…

…but a water dragon, asleep in the lake.

"They sleep all day and wake as the sun goes down," whispers Dad. Just then, the dragon opens one glowing yellow eye and looks around.

"Is it dangerous?" whispers Tora. "What if it swims over here and wants to eat us?"

"Don't worry. They're very gentle and only eat fish fingers."

Tora leans against her father and watches the water dragon for a long time. Please let it only eat fish fingers, she thinks.

"Good night, water dragon…"

"…and good night snake and giraffes and lion and hippos and trolls and fairies and scary crocodile…

And good night, best Dad in the world."

This edition first published in 2014 by Gecko Press
PO Box 9335, Marion Square, Wellington 6141, New Zealand
info@geckopress.com

Distributed in New Zealand by Random House NZ
Distributed in Australia by Scholastic Australia
Distributed in the United Kingdom by Bounce Sales & Marketing

First American edition published in 2014 by Gecko Press USA,
an imprint of Gecko Press Ltd.

Distributed in the United States and Canada by
Lerner Publishing Group, Inc.
241 First Avenue North
Minneapolis, MN 55401 USA
www.lernerbooks.com

A catalog record for this book is available from the US Library of Congress.

First published in Sweden by Bonnier Carlsen Bokförlaget, Stockholm, Sweden
Published in the English language by arrangement with Bonnier Carlsen Bokförlaget
Original title: *Se upp för krokodilen!*

The cost of this translation was defrayed by a subsidy from the
Swedish Arts Council, gratefully acknowledged.

A catalogue record for this book is available from the National Library of New Zealand

Translated by Julia Marshall
Edited by Penelope Todd
Typeset by Vida & Luke Kelly, New Zealand
Printed in China by Everbest Printing Co Ltd, an accredited ISO 14001 & FSC certified printer

ISBN hardback: 978-1-877579-89-9
ISBN paperback: 978-1-877579-90-5

For more curiously good books, visit www.geckopress.com